The King of the Birds

Malachy Doyle
Illustrated by Mike Terry

One morning all the birds of the air came to the Great Rock. They had a lot to talk about.

The proud eagle was the first to speak. "We need a king," he said, "a king of the birds."

"Yes," said the other birds, "you are right, Eagle. But how will we choose one?"

They talked and they talked until the sun rose high in the sky.

Some said that the goose should be king because he was the oldest.

Some said that the owl should be king because she was the wisest.

Some said that the bluejay should be king because he was the most colourful.

The proud eagle was not pleased. He thought that he should be king.

"I know who should be king," he said. "The bird who flies highest of all!"

And the others agreed. The little wren was sad to hear this. He wanted to be king, but he could fly no higher than the top of the bushes.

Now the wren was a clever little bird, and he had a plan.

While the other birds were talking, he crept under the eagle's tail feathers and hid in them. It was dark in there and no one could see him.

When it was time for the birds to fly, the blackbird took off first. She flew to the top of an old oak tree.

"From my tree top so tall, I can see all!" she cried.

"I can fly higher than that," said the lark. He took off from the top of the Great Rock. Soon he was gliding through the air, high above an old tower.

"Flying so high, I'm the king of the sky!" he cried.

"We can fly higher than that," said the other birds. They took off from the Great Rock, and the air was filled with birds of every kind. But no matter how hard they tried, none of them could fly higher than the lark.

When they returned to the Great Rock they cried: "The lark, the lark, is the king of the birds, for he can fly highest of all."

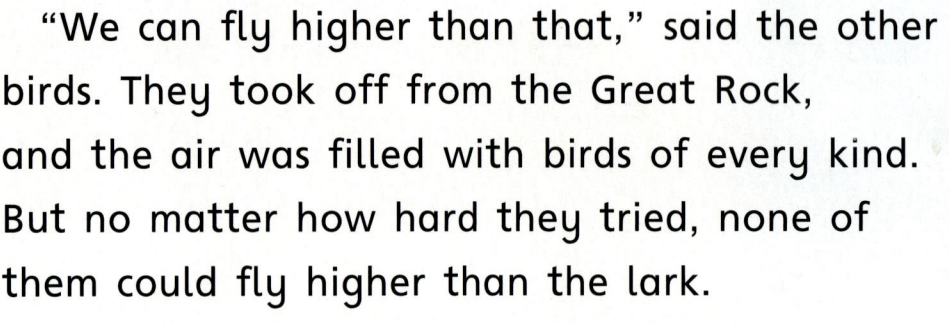

The proud eagle had not moved.
"Be quiet, you silly birds," he said.
"For I can fly higher than any of you."
And up he flew high into the air,
high above the Great Rock
and high above the oak tree,
high above the tower
and high above the mountain.
The eagle flew higher than any
bird had ever flown. Up he flew
almost as high as the sun!

"Beware, beware, I'm the king of the air!" he called.

But the proud eagle flew so high and stayed up so long that he became tired.

The eagle was about to come down when the wren flew out from under his tail.

The clever little bird had been hiding there all the time. He was waiting for the eagle to carry him into the sky, higher, much higher than he had ever flown before.

The wren opened his tiny wings and flew into the air above the eagle.

"I'm the wren, I'm the wren, I'm higher again!" he cried.

The proud eagle saw the wren above him and knew that he had lost. He tried to fly higher, but he was tired, too tired.

The eagle flew back down to the other birds, and the wren floated down behind him.

When the eagle landed on the Great Rock, the birds all cried:

"The eagle, he is king of the birds. He can fly highest of them all!"

For the wren was so high and so small that they had not seen him.

"I am not your king," said the eagle, sadly. "The wren is king, because he flew higher than I, and higher than any bird has ever flown!"

The birds rushed over to the tired little wren and crowned him king.

From that day on, though the clever wren never flew higher than the bushes, everyone knew that he was king of the birds.